The text has been translated and retold from the story "Baba Yaga"
published in the collection of Russian folktales compiled in the mid-nineteenth century by Aleksandr Afanas'ev

The art for this book was prepared first as black line drawings. These were used as guidelines for the
full-color art, which was painted with gouache on watercolor paper. The line drawings were then
photographed separately for greater contrast and sharpness.

Library of Congress Cataloging-in-Publication Data is available.
A CIP catalogue record for this book is available from The British Library.
ISBN 1-55858-287-8 (trade binding)
ISBN 1-55858-288-6 (library binding)

Designed by Marc Cheshire. Printed in Belgium.
1 3 5 7 9 10 8 6 4 2

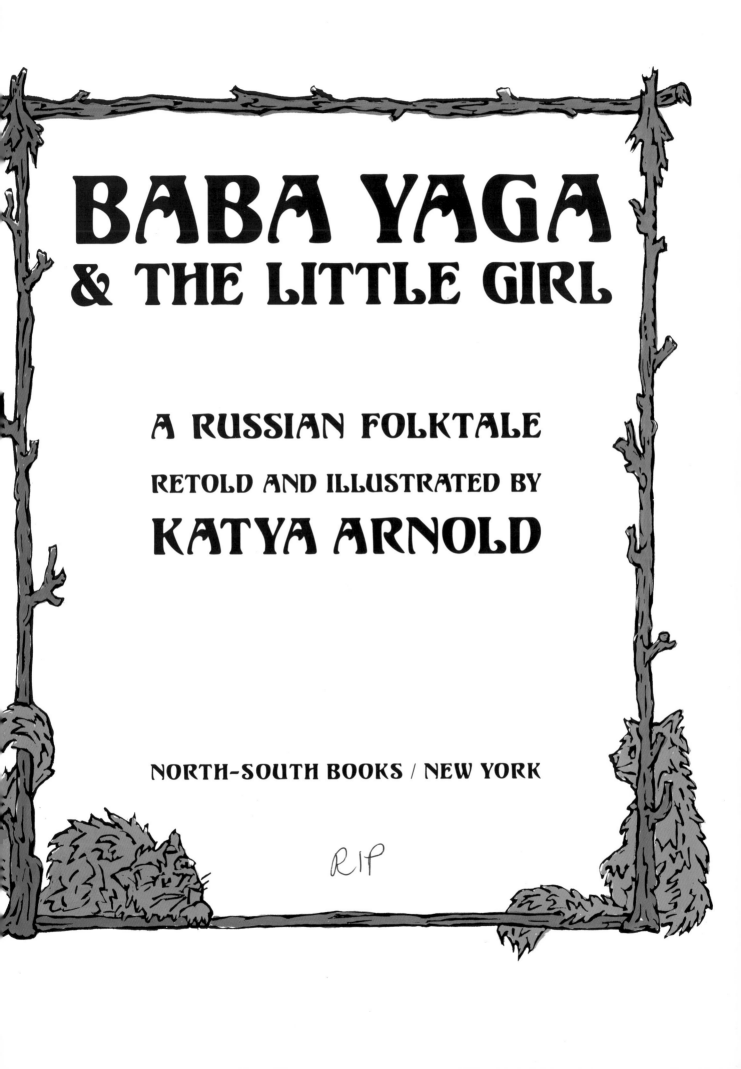

BABA YAGA
& THE LITTLE GIRL

A RUSSIAN FOLKTALE

RETOLD AND ILLUSTRATED BY
KATYA ARNOLD

NORTH-SOUTH BOOKS / NEW YORK

RIP

ONCE UPON A TIME there lived an old man and his wife and their little girl. They lived happily until the wife died and the old man got married again. The new wife was cruel and ugly and she immediately disliked the little girl. She cursed and beat her often and wanted to get rid of her forever.

So one day, when the father was away on a trip, the stepmother said to the little girl: "Go to my sister and ask her for a needle and some thread to sew a new shirt for your father." But the little girl was very clever, so she first went to see her own aunt.

"Good day, Auntie!"

"Good day, my beloved! Why are you so sad?"

"Stepmother sent me to her sister for a needle and thread to sew a shirt for my father."

"Don't be afraid, my dear," said her aunt. "Do as I tell you. When you get there, a birch will lash your eyes, so you should tie it up with a ribbon. The gates will bang and creak, so you should pour some oil on their hinges. The dogs will try to tear you apart, so you should feed them some bread. And a cat will try to scratch your eyes, so you should give him some ham. This is my advice."

The little girl thanked her aunt and walked and walked and walked until she came to a strange hut. And guess who the stepmother's sister was: Baba Yaga! The one who lives in the hut on chicken legs!

"Good day, Auntie!" said the little girl.

"Good day, my beloved!"

"Mother sent me for a needle and thread to sew a shirt."

"Very well," said Baba Yaga. "I'll give it to you, but in exchange you must work for me. Go into the hut and start knitting."

So the little girl started to work. Meanwhile Baba Yaga called her maid and said: "Bring some water from the well, heat it, and wash my niece. But wash her well—I want to eat her for dinner."

The little girl heard this and was scared to death. She begged the maid: "Dearest, don't make such a big fire! Don't burn so much wood!

Don't bring water in a bucket—bring it in a sieve!" And she gave the maid a beautiful kerchief.

Baba Yaga waited. She came to the window and asked: "Are you knitting, little niece? Are you knitting, my dearest?"

"Yes, I am knitting, Auntie. I am knitting, my dearest," she replied.

So Baba Yaga went away. The little girl gave ham to the cat and asked: "Dear cat! Can you help me escape? Baba Yaga wants to eat me."

"Here are a comb and a towel," said the cat. "Take them and run as fast as you can. I will knit for you until you get away. Baba Yaga will pursue you, but if you put your ear to the ground, you will hear her coming close. Just before she reaches you, throw the towel on the ground, and it will become a wide, wide river. And if Baba Yaga crosses that river and begins to catch up with you, put your ear to the ground again. When you hear her coming close, throw your comb on the ground, and it will become a very thick forest. She'll never, ever get through it."

The little girl thanked the cat, took the towel and the comb, and ran away.

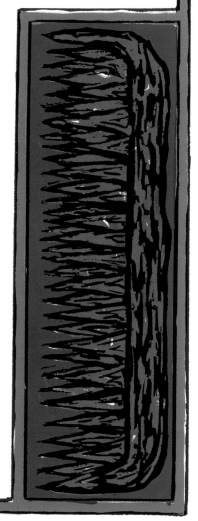

But at the gate wild dogs wanted to tear her apart, so she fed them some bread and they let her pass. Then the gates wanted to bang and creak, so she poured some oil on their hinges and they let her pass.

Then a birch tree wanted to lash her eyes, so she tied it with a ribbon and it let her pass.

Meanwhile the cat was supposed to be knitting, but he started to chase the ball of yarn around the room and got it all tangled and wrapped around everything.

Baba Yaga crept up to the window and asked: "Are you knitting, my niece? Are you knitting, my dearest?"

"Yes, I am knitting, Auntie. I am knitting, my dearest," answered the cat in his thick, rough voice.

Baba Yaga rushed into the hut and saw that the little girl was gone. She cursed and thrashed the cat, and scolded him for not having scratched out the girl's eyes.

"I served you for many years and you never gave me even a bone," said the cat, "but she gave me a piece of ham."

Baba Yaga rushed out to catch the little girl, but the girl was already gone. Baba Yaga was so angry that she crushed the gate, tore the branches off the birch, grabbed the maid by her hair, and thrashed the dogs.

The dogs whined: "We served you for many years and you never threw us even a crumble of bread, but that girl gave us a whole loaf!"

The gates squeaked: "We served you for many years and you never even poured grease on our hinges, but that girl poured pure oil!"

The birch tree rustled: "I served you for many years and you never even tied me with thread, but that girl tied my branches with a beautiful ribbon!"

As Baba Yaga jumped in her mortar and pushed it through the woods with her pestle, the maid cried out after her: "I served you for many years and you never gave me even a rag, but that girl gave me a lovely kerchief!"

After running and running and running, the little girl put her ear to the ground and heard Baba Yaga chasing her in the mortar. She was coming closer and closer.

So the little girl threw down the towel, and it became a wide, rapid river. Baba Yaga came to the river, but she could not cross it. So she just gnashed her teeth in helpless rage.

Baba Yaga returned home, took her oxen, and drove them to the river. The mighty oxen drank up all the water in the river, and Baba Yaga continued her chase.

The little girl felt the earth shaking and put her ear to the ground. She heard Baba Yaga coming closer and closer. So the little girl threw the comb over her shoulder and it became a dense dark forest. Baba Yaga started to gnaw through the trees, but she broke all her teeth and was forced to go back to her hut on chicken legs.

Meanwhile the little girl's father returned home from his trip and asked: "Where is my little girl? Why is she not greeting me?"

"She has gone to her aunt and has not yet returned," replied his wicked wife. "I fear that something may have happened to her."

Just then the little girl came running home—all pale and tired.

"Where have you been so long, my little girl?" asked her father.

"Oh, Father dear," gasped the little girl. "My stepmother sent me to her sister for a needle and thread to sew you a new shirt, but her sister was Baba Yaga—and she wanted to eat me!"

"But how did you escape, my poor darling?"

The little girl told him the whole story.

When her father heard what really happened to his daughter, he got very, very angry and threw his wife out. Then the little girl made him a beautiful shirt with the needle and thread she had brought from Baba Yaga. They lived happily ever after and were never bothered by Baba Yaga again.